The
Return

Kevin Boileau

also by Kevin Boileau

Literary

A Reason and A Season

The Patient

The Blue Pearl

Abject Poverty

99 Deceptions

The Separation

Coming Soon

The Bishop... A Fisherman

3 Rivers

Outlaw Series

Theory

Genuine Reciprocity and Group Authenticity
First Edition

Genuine Reciprocity and Group Authenticity:
The Social Ontology of Sartre & Foucault

The Algebra of History (*with David A. Boileau*)

Essays on Phenomenology and the Self

Manifesto on Solidarity; Ethics for a New World

Coming Soon

The Psychoanalytic Approach to Mediation

EPIS Press
31 Fort Missoula Road, Suite 4
Missoula, MT 59804 USA
epispublishing1@gmail.com
www.episworldwide.com

Heart-of-Fire is an imprint of
EPIS Press

The Heart-of-Fire name and logo
are trademarks of EPIS Press

Printed in the United States of America
Library of Congress
1. Psychoanalysis 2. Psychology 3. Phenomenology
4. Spirituality 5. Death 6. Separation 7. Morality

Cover Design: Tia Hopkins
Author Photo: NTG
Author Seal: Adrian Balasa

ISBN 978-0-9849512-6-0

THE
RETURN

by
Kevin Boileau

FIRST
PART

1st Chapter

From a journal entry:

We'd heard the news that he was returning, living life much the same as we had before he was gone. We were slowly evolving, which would allow greater freedom of choice in our programs but he was still under the old rules. This meant that the details of his assignment had been chosen without his participation and that he was under contract to comply.

Under the rules we would hear from him through the report system at the end of each "year," which made us all feel good to know he was safe and well.

Since the last "Council," we had all been caught between the old and the new, but time was timeless. Most of our historians and archaeologists had been digging into the genesis of our cultural weltanschauung, but no one really knew about it other than the fragments that were archived in libraries. This is why it was easy to see time as timeless—there were no fixed temporal points.

We had a big house that had been in the family for several generations. It was compound-style, so any of us could come and go without disrupting the flow for everyone else. His cottage had sat vacant for a while until we decided to use it for a private art gallery, a guest house, empty space, a retro-version of his space, a meeting forum, and then back to the way it was when he left. We had a cleaning crew come monthly.

No one knew when he'd be back, exactly, but in the late afternoons I would sit with his cat on the green grass staring into the sun as it dipped down into the mountains.

2nd Chapter

He was getting ready. I could see it in the lightness of his expression, which had come after the fatigue and the pain. He had lived completely, and had fully played his part, which was now coming to a close.

He had walked with stiffness for the last few years but it seemed unbelievably gone. Any resentment that he had carried also seemed to have dissipated. As such, there was nothing in his voice that carried emotional valence: there was only the softness of his blue eyes and the compassionate detachment that come from total release.

He often talked about friends from the old days, and when he wasn't doing this he made comments about what would come next. He didn't seem to know and didn't speculate, and as such was fully inside the ontological bloom of transformation.

I tried to reach him during this time, the late December of his life, but didn't succeed. I wanted the sort of mutuality that friends enjoy, sharing comments that would never leave an inner sanctum of trust and loyalty. I didn't receive them, didn't experience them, and did not get what I wanted. But I lingered in the hope, and waited around for something to happen, which eventually did.

He was tall, big. Strong.

He had blue eyes, like I said. They were smart blue eyes that twinkled with wisdom, and humor. They were blue eyes that had bounced back from pain. They were blue eyes that would remain. His gait was more of a shuffle in his last few years on account of his bad hips. He grimaced when he moved but tried to keep this to himself.

He was getting ready to return, eighty-odd years into the lesson—enough had been learned. For complicated reasons he had been unable to communicate with them—those he had left—except in his heart, but he was certain that they knew.

~ ~ ~

We were at the funeral up on the hill at the southeast side of town, which had a good view of the sun especially at the end of the day when it turned to dusk. We were all there. Somewhere else far away there was another family—

It was sunny and the skies blue, like usual in our town. It was quiet up here on the knoll where they'd built the new graveyard. Everyone had come, the locals and the others from out of town, to say goodbye. He had been well liked, so everyone was flexible and amiable about the event.

"Is it time?" one of us had asked, just before the funeral a little while ago. Then we all piled into the three or four cars at the house to get to the church. After the sayings we then headed to up there to the edge of town following the long, black car.

It was warm, especially in the car, so I was glad when we went into the church and even more glad at the grassy space at the top of the hill. There was a light wind, nearly imperceptible, which continued to move the sweaty stress off into the distance toward the mountains.

We grouped into a semi-circle facing the pastor while he said the important words, some of which I'd heard before. Today, however, they struck me differently because it hit close to home. I'd remembered the time years ago when we talked about this sort of thing. He had made it clear that after he jumped into the water the current would take him beyond my grasp and soon enough everything would be different.

Today he was still here close, intermixing with the imperceptible wind. In the past several decades he'd gone from being my father to my friend, and then back to being my father. Toward the end I saw him as a fellow traveler, on a path I could never fully understand, but this did not detract from the love I felt for him. In the end, he'd been the best teacher I'd ever had; in quiet moments I considered whether I would have been as good to him, roles reversed.

3rd Chapter

I was excited for the weekend because we were going hiking into the lakes—just the two of us—and it felt like a coming of age. I'd been through survival training, read the outdoor books, and got Him to buy me the gear, so I was ready. We left early in the week, just the two of us, and got to the trailhead by the time the sun broke. He had the lunch, the fishing poles, and extra everything if we needed.

We walked solid for several hours, talking about the mundane and the superficial, occasionally broaching the philosophical, intermixed with the light thudding of our boots on the dirt trail, until we made our way in elevation to the first lake. There we stopped, drank water, shared a sandwich, and enjoyed the blue skies.

We fished without success for the mountain trout and then walked higher into a constellation of several other lakes, late in the afternoon, sweat dripping off our foreheads, working our reels as the warmth receded and the dusk took over. We each caught one, and shortly we both enjoyed crackling flames, coffee, and the fish.

We did this for 3 days, then on the 4th his mood changed. He said he had to go away and that it had all been arranged. He had brought me here to "to explain things."

The 4th night, fire crackling, stars filling the sky, tents up. Mountain Lake—gurgling intermittently, between the quick-second lives of each dancing orange-yellow.

"It will soon be time for me to go away." [I will never

forget those words—they still stuck with me even through the many revolutions of things since then.]

It took us long into the night until he was able to get me to accept that he would be leaving me, all of us, but he wanted to tell me on his own—man to man.

As he spoke on into the night my vision propelled itself into the illusion, mirage, and fantasy of the gleaming, shining white dots in the black.

—Leaving.

—Going away.

—Telling me in the dark.

My father.

~ ~ ~

The next day we broke camp and hiked further to the highest lake. This was where the snow was pure-white, clean, and unadulterated. We set the packs down and took in the mountain air, which was cool and protective, far away from the city below. We both shared a drink of good whiskey even though it was not quite noon. He pulled out a cigarette—one that he had been saving— and took a couple of puffs on it before offering it to me. Even though I normally didn't smoke or drink, there was something about the combination mixed with the high air that was intoxicating in a mind-full way.

We were beginning some sort of ritual, to be sure, so I relaxed into it, trusting Him for whatever came next.

It was the readings. He pulled out a couple of books, pages marked, and read as the rest of the cigarette burned down on the dirt. He took another sip from the bottle of spirits and then continued, drawing attention to this part and that, gesticulating until he was done.

The fullness of the foggy air had been fragmented and separated by the rays of sun angling their way over the top of the ridge, disappearing in the top part of the green-brown tree line. Bellies full of coffee and bread, the fulcrum of the tension between the receding nothingness of the air that became unlimited sky, and the heavy dirt pack of the trail that had gotten us here.

–Your mother and I have talked it all over and we're good.

–We have had a wonderful journey together.

–My life, here, has been good to me. There are many things I still do not understand but it is time for me to go.

–[Go where? I questioned.] What do you mean?

–I brought you here to say goodbye, son. I have to go. It's time.

I had no basis for understanding other than Grandma's funeral and the friends I left when we moved out of the old neighborhood, so I was perplexed. "Have to go?" What's that?

He went on to explain–succinctly–that there was much to learn and that things are not always what they seem. We had about an hour more together, he shared, and then he would be leaving this life. He explained something about transformation, which I didn't understand, wondered if I could carry both packs, and then motioned to the lake just above and to the west which cascaded into a stream that would wind its way deep into the forest on the other side.

He encouraged me to trust in the way of things. He expressed that everything was all right—perfect—just the way it was and we should celebrate his departure just as much as the time we shared. He reminded me how I had tasted innocence as a boy, and had spit it out as repugnant to the truth. This sharing brought great relief in me, as we walked down to the lake, perhaps thirty feet or so away, partially obscured by the remaining mist, the fir and pine, and the small mountain scrub, moss, and shale rock that overflowed onto the land.

We sat together and talked longer. Then we stopped and shared the silence sitting at the end of the noon hour. He muttered something about everything "happening all at once" and that what would be was already. This, I did not understand, but I would remember it always. He requested that I sit here for fifteen minutes and thank the ground where we had sat, then to walk down the mountain to what would be.

I watched him disrobe, almost while he was walking into the cold water until he disappeared. Then I burned his clothes as he had directed, giving thanks to our campsite; then I headed down toward town.

4th Chapter

Days before he passed away we were all stuffing our face with grease at the Double-Front Chicken—mashed potatoes, gravy, a medley of deep-fried chicken pieces and Coca-Cola—until we'd had our fill of each other. Then we ended our reunion and everyone left for home. I remember watching his face as he squeezed himself into the car. He'd been watching the rain clear up in the west and seemed pleased that the sun was peering out so late in the day. It'd been good to see him, and everyone else, but enough was enough with family, and I was happy to go home without an extra beer or dessert.

I had an out-of-town trip that week and heard about it when I was at the hotel at night, a good three hours away. It wasn't surprising—he was old and his time and come over and over with narrow escapes—and I was ready, so we put it all in motion. I'd walked past the mortuary since I was a little boy, now with decades of imaginings about what was inside. This was the planning part, the transition of feelings and alliances as extended family re-balanced itself for the future, and everyone cooperated like you'd expect at an assembly line, except that it was a one-shot deal.

By the time we had the funeral (which was really nice for me because I hadn't been inside there since I was a teenager) and ended up at the knoll at one end of the grassy cemetery, we were ready for it to be over. Enough tears, food [more chicken], and family conversations, had tired everyone out and we were all operating on adrenalin. Thus, we welcomed the little bluff at the edge of the grass, especially because it was quiet with blue skies, and a light breeze had stirred up as cars arrived.

After everything became still, we heard the words about shadows and valleys, which I never entirely understood because of my predilection for sun and light. I took a couple of family members with me, on the unlikely route over the old Mullan Bridge and came up to the place from the backside. We creeped up in the big car away from everyone else which gave us a different perspective on things that didn't include the noise and all the people. I quickly separated from everyone and walked through the grass alone [it was a large cemetery and park with benches]. I squeezed a picture I had of him when he was a boy and took it out, blocking out the sun so I could how he looked when he was a boy. There was that innocence, and it appeared that he hadn't spit it out as repugnant, which made me smile: he'd always been good at hiding things from others and from himself. Then I approached the group.

We listened to the formal words that were always said. Then a few of the immediate family, not including myself, said some personal words, but this was all kept short because everyone had just gotten the chance to speak in the church. But there were a few remaining things to say like "Be well, my friend" or "We'll always love you." For others, it was a few more tears or an acknowledgment with a nod. I'd had enough midway into it, and so I started drifting back a few steps until I was at the periphery of the group. I was right in the interstitial place between the people and the hard-packed dirt and grass of the cemetery. I was right in the middle place where I could hear both the pastor and the cars in the parking lot filled with people talking. I was in the ambivalent place where I was both here and not here at the same time.

Then a movement caught my eye. It was off to one of the edges of the green area, near the benches. It was quiet now while everyone watched the box being lowered. It was dead silence in the parking lot as if everyone knew about the solemnity of the lowering.

I tried not to jerk my head in an obvious say so I wouldn't distract the group, but I could see him in the periphery of my sight toward the far end of the place. Because everyone's eyes were bent downwards as they listened to the religious words, and because the group was big enough, no one noticed as I slipped back to the very last row.

By now the casket was closed and sealed and was sinking into the ground with the ropes and the burial contraption.

He had appeared on the edge of the lawn and I could see him standing there facing away, his head turned toward us. No one noticed him except for me.

He looked serene, quiet, peaceful, a soft smile on his face, his eyes twinkling. He could see me looking at him, and we held our mutual gaze. Normally, you'd expect that I'd be seriously unsettled, but I wasn't. Something about the light wind intermixing with his image down at the end of the cemetery, the green grass and the blue skies, and the gentle words of the pastor, made all possibilities real. As such, anyone could have appeared and it would not have bothered me. This is to say that it was a day of openings and not questions.

He was standing there, poised to leave. Then he sat for a moment on the bench there—in the stillness—his eyes still peering at us with gratitude. He looked at us standing there, to the sun, around to the mountains, and then back to me.

It was dreamlike for me, and allowed me to access the memory of a dog I had loved many years prior. He had been old and stiff like my father, and I had facilitated his merciful passing before burying his body in the ground. I say that I had buried "his body" instead of "him" because I learned that night the difference.

After the tears and the emptiness had fallen into smarting, wistful fatigue, and I had fallen asleep, I dreamed. The little dog's spirit had climbed out of the dirt, skirted the house, and in the middle of the night in the dark, left us. When he had gotten to the front of the house—and keep in mind that it was pitch black except for the moon—he had looked around in confusion, no longer recognizing his once familiar home. Then he trotted off heading north, paying close attention, walking just next to the curb, directed elsewhere. It was clear in the dream, which upon reflection was my acute access to the truth, that he had somewhere else to be, that he no longer recognized his family.

As he skipped away—I felt so much love for him my heart was bursting with joy—I realized that the identity he had taken on in his lifetime was for us. It was temporally conditioned, and once over, unremembered. His greater reality—soul, self, anima, life force, or whatever you want to call it—was in a different dimension with a deep purpose and a deep, abiding motive. A few days later when I went to his grave, the dirt still upturned from where they had jabbed the shovel into the earth, it felt empty. I had an urge to dig him out and to breathe life back into him but the horror that fantasy caused stopped me short.

I wanted to be the dirt.

I remember looking at his gravesite one last time, and I have never been back there since. I doubt I ever will but it doesn't matter because I took it with me. It was in me.

Once I had replayed my memory of the dog, which took place in perhaps two or three seconds, my consciousness moved back to the gaze of my father who had died just three days before, and whose body was being lowered into the cold ground capped by the warming sun as it probed into the grass. Back and forth three times I looked at him then at the burial scene–to them and back. He smiled, letting me know clearly that everything was all right, not to fear any of it.

It was very quiet now, a hawk flying overhead, very high; the few clouds that remained were receding; what cars had been there seemed to have left. No one except me had noticed him, which was an engaging insight I would ponder for a long time. It was just them in the ceremony, me at the back periphery, and him–looking.

Though I wanted this moment to linger; though it was hard to let it end; though the burial was nearly over; though I was alone in this with him; though the sun would not last; though I could feel my stomach hungry; though I did not understand–

I said goodbye; not with words or gestures. It was with my eyes. He smiled one last time and as my view was temporarily diverted by the pastor's final words and the high-flying hawk that had spotted a rabbit. I looked away for less than a second and back in his direction but he was gone. He had disappeared into the brown sagebrush at the end of the cemetery that went on from one field bleeding into the next until they met up with the rolling hills and the river, and then the sky.

The grieving family members and close friends paid their final respects with quiet, subtle acknowledgements. Then they left, the coffin in its resting place, open to the sky, the process finished. They left quietly; I waited until they were gone, half expecting the little dog to trot across the cemetery; or that he would re-appear with another message. There was none, and after the breeze kicked up and the sun disappeared behind the quickly forming rain clouds. Then I left, making my way back the same way, re-crossing the bridge. I left town the next morning.

5th Chapter

Things had operated pretty much the same way for a long time since we had settled into the Valley. Although some of the original manuscripts had been lost, there was enough of the original Architecture and Philosophy to accommodate new cultural developments. At least I had heard of the original sayings, even though I had not actually ever seen them. Summers were endless here, hot, with a humming sound that would begin just after noon and continue until after dinner. Winters were similar, with snowfields that glistened and which sang a lullaby, one that you could hear if you focused on it. The lullaby of the snow was like the harmony to the summer humming. Fall and spring were purely transformative.

Another journal entry:

[After he left, we learned that the Committee and the local Proctor had required it. This was something serious but details were sketchy so there was a lot of innuendo and guesswork. Unfortunately, his leaving had caused various social and familial stresses and folks had to re-arrange a number of matters. To top that off, he-himself was not pleased in having to leave: he'd done everything required of him and was neck-deep into a number of commitments.

However, there had been an infraction and, as such, there would be a penalty and a learning. This was the way of our world in those days and so he was one of the last ones to go through the process.

We all saw him off as he entered the Time & Space Holograph and left us for an undetermined period. It took a while then things shifted into memory and hope, and the managing of his space. I was aware of all these things because I was old—I'd been around for a long time—and I knew how things were.

There'd been an event and someone had been harmed. A baby had been lost and she had been escorted from town, both of them. Then he was forced into service and eventually made to leave. This was after the preparation, which included leaving everything, including one's personal identity and body at the final travel bins. Then you'd have to go through this process, which was complex and difficult to explain, before you were sent on a multi-dimensional journey to the learning space. It was known as "Earth."

On his journey day, we congregated at the family compound and celebrated the time we'd all had together, uncertain about when he'd return and what that might bring. Little was said about the behavior that had triggered all this to happen, and mostly we focused on small, familial chuckles and gratitude. Myself, I'd been around a long time, and I hoped that there would be no inter-dimensional reprisal and that all would go smoothly until the return.

Because of my seniority, occasionally I had access to private files and reports, and I was also curious about his status. Much, much time had passed since I'd watched him go away, and in the spring I'd hike to the lake into which he had disappeared. I noticed throughout the years that the snow had melted quite a bit, which filled the lake fuller; but I also knew that with the changing climate patterns, eventually all of the snow would melt and eventually the lake would dry up. This was the way of things.]

I continued on as usual, had my own obligations, my

own learning, and my own traveling, which took me to many inter-dimensional destinations. My memory of him remained unfettered although it receded and surfaced without any sort of pattern. More curiously, I experienced a significant inability to find myself when a) I tried or b) I would come home from a travel. The "me" I would run into was a facsimile of my former self, a simulacra of the memory I had of myself, such discrepancy causing me a bit of feeling unsettled. This always led to a weird sort of wistfulness about the "way things had been" instead of focusing on the future or my immediate needs.

I felt this way about my father, who by now, had been gone for many revolutions of the sun—through many seasons as this experience of returning to a distorted image of myself. The memory helped anchor me as I traveled further and further from my point of origin, on occasion losing my way and sometimes "forgetting" to presence the memory. As such, "return" became an exercise in ontological security, but only if I had been particularly disoriented by the project.

As I aged, I realized how hard we each tried to maintain the semblance and integrity of a "self" even though we were constantly pulled back into the dirt of the land. We lived in the abject, all of us, even though we deceived ourselves into believing that we could attain nihilist transcendence from it. Unfortunately, these frenetic attempts at transcendence were often more destructive than not, and I finally allowed myself to sink back into my origin more often than not.

I was on my own spirit journey, too, and took assignments regularly though they amounted to short-term prospects that did not involve loss of consciousness or my self-identity. However, I kept the important memories intact, including some of my pivotal times growing up. I'd go back to the family home from time to time, and would inevitably spend a few minutes sitting in his room, wondering if he were going to show up again. I grew older. My hair turned gray. I lost my youth. Still, he didn't come.

Sometimes I'd go to the cemetery where we had buried him, sitting in front of the gravestone, talking, talking, talking, but this was not fruitful. Then I began to doubt that I had actually seen him leaving the cemetery during the burial. I chalked it up to grief. I called to him: no answer. I looked to the edge of the grassy knoll where he'd smiled at me: nothing there. It was only sun, blue skies, and grass in the summer; clouds, chill, and brown in the winter. My life went on—no resolution from him.

SECOND PART

6th Chapter

I still didn't fully understand why I had been directed
to go on this journey—which would be for an indefinite
amount of time, and a lack of clear understanding
about my purpose. After I left home I was ushered into a
series of "preparations and preliminaries" from which I
would begin this interminable lesson.

That had been a long time ago, and I am only writing
about it now because at the time I was no longer aware
of the journey. I was just on it. Just recently I figured out
that I had been taken from my "real" life and made to
go somewhere else, in a different time, with different
expectations, truths, and realities.

After I had been here for a while, I started spending
more time in the cemeteries, which fascinated and
intrigued me. I was drawn to them.

When I had first arrived, the shame I carried from the
infraction was palpable, present, and heavy in my daily
life. According to the plan, no one here would know,
but that didn't take away from my own burden.

Earlier today I was in the old graveyard that they'd
started when the town was first settled. I walked the
grounds, stopping at the various stones intermittently,
in the space of an hour going from snow to sunshine
and clear skies. Not all the gravesites had clearly-
marked names, and others were disintegrating into the
ground with leaves and dirt covering what some caring
person had placed there so many years ago.

It was both puzzling and intriguing that my last name

was written all over at least a dozen of the graves. I talked to the groundskeeper. I got a map to all the sites—the ones that had records. I did some research. But though I was joined in name with these people, I felt no kinship. Even after I learned of some of their stories—their struggles, their triumphs—I felt nothing. Maybe this is why I continued to return over and over.

Today, it was now blue skies and sun. Because I was a reporter for the local paper, I had access to all the usual history and research in the valley, which I used frequently. I was part of a family, had a wide and children, friends, and a "history." This way I could locate the meaning of my narrative trajectory.

I had finally integrated my ontological possibilities with my actual life until they seemed totally convergent and co-extensive. I was just who I was and no longer considered another life with another set of possibilities. In sum, I had fully eased into what had been laid out for me, and all the other fantasies, imaginations, and speculations were over. That is, until I got the call.

This was just a few days ago, when I was on my way late to work, mid-morning, after having spent more time in the graveyard. I recognized the voice instantly. It was the same person who had called me a long time ago to tell me I had to leave. The message was similar: I needed to make preparations for the return. They would be calling me again soon with details. He also said that they would be repeating instructions because the transition required radical adjustment, which could take some doing.

Obviously this was an ontological rupture of profound proportions, opening up a fissure in my being that put everything into question.

[It put everything into question. Thus, it felt incumbent on me to figure out the 'why', perhaps correct it, or go into the new with some semblance of control. In the alternative, I could stop caring about what was happening, eager for the morrow. Later in the evening I realized I could be okay with the nothingness of the interstitial corridor between the old and new, appreciating the open, transcendent space in which all things were possible. I was being informed that my narrative trajectory—one that I had come to love in its familiarity—would soon end. This is not to say that I would cease to exist, for that would be a different result, but that I would have to 'pack my bags' so to say and head for uncharted waters. More complicated was how this would all play out socially. I had a family and I couldn't tell them I'd be soon gone. That was part of the deal.]

"When does this all happen?"

"Don't worry about that—we will let you know. Right now you should begin to make preparations. We will send a list. The main thing is to be ready."

That afternoon, then, I experienced a significant shift in my relationships, even with my wife. In a way, the details were not important; what was more momentous was that my existential experience had shifted—I was torn from what had become a familiar and comfortable life—in which all matters were expected. This, of course, had created in me a space of safety. It was a practical convergence between the actual and the possible.

I headed out to Mullan Country Road to get to the plateau where I could park.

On the way my mind oscillated between the imagination of the sea and the reality of the brown, dry dirt. It had been a long time since I had been to the coast, and I'd all but forgotten the smell: mountain flowers here had almost completely assimilated the memory.

I got there midday and sat. The hills from the west were close, green-brown because the summer wasn't over. From the east they were like backyard pets, so they became part of your everyday life. But the hills from the west were more like weekend or seasonal friends—you'd only notice them when you drove out here on the country roads, out on the plateau that led to the West River.

They'd built a golf course out here so some of the gentry from out of town had moved in, but mostly it was still the same combination of plains and plateaus upon which the railroad had carried hundreds of thousands until the big money dried up. As such, you could still see the brown-red trestles snaking out of the canyon to the east and heading into toward the deep-green forests in the west. Other than that, there was just brown dirt, sagebrush, and a multitude of gopher holes—little heads poking their heads into the sky for the latest information. This is where I parked the car, waiting for him.

Since I was out there along, I got out of my car, an old blue Fairlane, and smoked an Indian-made cigarette as the sun drifted across the early afternoon sky atop of the mountains that were the backdrop for the closer, watching hills. I could see him approaching in the distance, so I put my communion with those close hills on hold.

The smoke rose out of the up and down of the car as it made its way westward from town, nosing its way left and right until it pulled up in a waft of smoke floating upward from the gray-brown dirt into the sky, pushed eastward by the giant air currents.

After I told him that I would be "going away" he was perplexed because I was unable to give him an adequate explanation. The best I could do was to say something about "destiny" and "transformation," but it wasn't enough. We reminisced about the old days when we'd first met and talked about the future, but this wasn't enough to keep him from asking about suicide. It's not that he said that that word, but he alluded to enough of the connotations for me to ask.

My response that it was more complicated than that confused the situation even more, but I think we ended with the meta-text that I wouldn't always be around, which he chalked up to sentimentality or some vague plan that I couldn't yet share. In the end, we shared the beauty of the surrounding mountains and the watchful hills, which we'd both played in as boys. He drove off and then I did, those hills looking—watching.

7th Chapter

I received a list in the mail. It contained the things I had to do in order to prepare for my return. There were three of them. I sat with the letter on the porch; I went to the park with it; I read it again at night. The first was easy: I was to outline everything I had learned and then commit to unlearning it; the second was to solve a riddle; the third was to discover a hidden artifact on the Mountain (this was the spiritual place near the river).

The riddle: *The man who dies before he dies does not die when he dies.* This I think I had read in a book but it seemed like a dream.

The unlearning: I wasn't sure I had ever learned anything so this troubled me.

The artifact: Though I knew the mountain well it was misty and tricky, so even with the clues to finding the directions, I was uncertain. I did not yet know what the object was or its significance.

I had no idea when the return would be scheduled but it was requested that I prepare forthwith with diligence. It seemed imminent so I began contemplating.

It was evident that there were forces in the universe about which I was unaware. I had been accelerated into a life not of my choosing, only to be asked to join another one, and then to leave—without explanation or reason. It was an exercise in faith to be asked these things, and then to comply without hesitation, but this time was difficult. In fact, I had been feeling a loss of my memory in various forms, and I'd started wondering how much had really been past. *How many times had I been asked to make the return?* I didn't know, but it felt like I was on the verge of a new discovery.

This gave me the impetus I needed for the three tasks. As such, I set out to contemplate the unlearning. This required a philosophical inquiry into the meaning of "learning," for I'd have to figure this out before I could seriously "unlearn" anything. I wasn't sure if the purpose was to make my journey easier, creating a temporal fluidity so that I could travel more easily; on the other hand, perhaps it was an ironic exercise the reason for which involved comedic perspective. We live. We die. We learn, we unlearn. I set about this task by visiting the town cemetery—not the one on the knoll but the one down in the old part.

This involved mornings with coffee, afternoons falling asleep to the sun, poking around looking for buried treasure, writing in a journal, and wandering aimlessly— working diligently toward the unlearning. Then I received another missive, instructing me to locate the artifact.

After several days of interpreting clues, hoofing it around the area, and using my compass, I located the box. It was cedar, wrapped and sealed in a small plastic bag, and buried up on the mountain. By the time I found the area—perhaps a two-acre square filled with cattle bones and light shrub, I was sweating though the sun had gone down. I found the spot and dug it up, unwilling to wait, so I pulled the bag off and opened it. The box was small so there was nowhere to hide but it was strange to me that there was only a small piece of square paper. There was nothing on it. This conundrum led me to the riddle.

Apparently, I had been living in a different dimension

before I'd been ordered here without my assent. Because I was directed to return there I had to "die" here first. I had learned the intimate connection between mind and body, so I created an illness in my body, which resulted in my "death."

Then they set the ceremony where they'd "bury" my body, and I'd be free to go. I had no idea how far I'd gotten with the unlearning, and I never understood the blank paper. The riddle meant nothing to me.

Awake again, tired and unkempt. Always dragging myself from that north side cemetery back to town. The repetition never got to me because each time there was slight variation. It could be in the way I walked, the attitude I chose, the things I saw, or merely in the small variations that it took—including the walk past the old 2-story house with the window. Sometimes I sensed that I was being watched, but it was so close to the cemetery that perhaps I was carrying with me the lingering gaze of the dead.

These strong feelings, happening over and over, finally got me to notice a reality deeper than the shiny, narrow one that I had previously fashioned. As I traversed the three requirements—the unlearning, the blank note, and the riddle, I wandered through town daily. The sun cut through me like a knife, opening me up to greater uncertainties about my journey. I had not only been tipped over, I had been pulled apart from myself—from the 'me' that I thought I had owned. Now I knew this wasn't true.

One day I stopped at the edge of one of the rivers, sat down and stopped what I was doing. It was an All-Stop kind of day—warm, sunny, slow. I was still in denial that I had to leave. This is not to say that I didn't understand I would be leaving, but there is a wide gap between understanding and existential saturation. I felt traces of wistfulness—that sort of sadness that one projects into the future-looking back: a future-oriented retrospective. It was all in the imaginary realm.

I went through the motions, so to speak, with my designated family and friends. It was difficult to hide what I was going through, but it was something I had to deal with on my own. This was a commandment from the universe—not to drag anyone into my return.

Sitting on the riverbank was not enough, so I rolled onto my back, enjoying an admixture of the gurgling and the soft swirling of the faint clouds that winked at me, inviting me into an unknown dance. I woke up hours later to rain and impending darkness. Such was the way in these parts of the country.

Thus, I plunged myself into the preparations for my imminent departure. In seeking the unlearning, the answer to the riddle, and the response to the blank, white paper, I was able to start pulling—well ripping really—myself away from the ontological constellation I called "myself."

Departing without warning was different from a preparatory illness that gave everyone notice. So I made myself sick, deep in my core, solely as an exercise in compassion. The reason would provide meaning for those I had to leave. So I got sick and everyone understood, when they figured out that I would pass away.

I realized in due course that I would write a message on the piece of paper and re-bury the cedar box before I left. I figured it was my moral duty to share something of my experience with someone in the future—perhaps my own.

The unlearning was, ironically, not something I could "do" in the sense of manifesting intentionality. Instead, I could understand it as a process of releasement even though my ability in that area was not strong. This set me to pondering why we attach ourselves to various truths and knowledges. It was possessory, yet in the possession we enslaved ourselves. In order to make the return I needed to let go of these attachments and instead focus on my deeper nature, which was ineluctable openness, perennial nihilation. I knew that I had to release myself from the possessory attachments in order to expose that openness. It was here in this space that I would find the portal to carry me home.

This made me question the authenticity of choices I had made during my time here. I considered the possibility that I had never made an original choice during this time, or anywhere else—that there was nothing "original" in my life, or anyone else's. Instead there was just what we did with our situations. If this were true, then futility only came from being overly attached to any sort of personal identity, for these were just working agreements with society—there wasn't anything else.

I didn't enjoy feeling forced into this releasement. However, I was grateful for the perspective I was being afforded between what was and what could be. It was that gap that I had lost over the years, and I was able to enjoy the nothingness of it.

One thing was becoming clear: that when you stand in the perspective of a certain construction of reality, that's what you see. Everything outside of that perspective seems foreign. However, when you shift perspectives, the same logic applies to the new perspective. Right now, I was operating from the perspective of the life I was living. Returning to a place I hadn't been to in a long time created a consciousness of "here and there."

This created a sense of movement in me that I had not known for a very long time.

8th Chapter

I had just driven out of the old City Cemetery—again—
(I had been there earlier in the day) and was shaken
when an old mean dog came out behind a fence and
snapped. He had meant business, I could tell, because
even my passing by didn't faze him. He just stuck to
his task undaunted, and I could see him gazing at me
even a block away. It was enough to jerk me out of the
reverie of the quiet necropolis and my goal for the day
of "practice writing" a message for the white piece of
paper in the cedar box.

After almost sideswiping three cars parked on the side
of the narrow road [All of them were smaller on account
of being in the older section of town.] I managed a
coffee at a drive-through and headed for the post office.

There was a note explaining that I was being afforded
the option to stay here in this world, not to return.

Instead of heeding them, I headed out to one of the
rivers. This was the dangerous one that could take your
life if you didn't respect it. Newer city houses blended
into larger, dilapidated ones, weeds grown over the
riverbanks, weeds grown over my head—dangling in my
eyes across my brow.

But the phlegm in my throat did not go away: the dog
had scared the hell out of me, and it was more than
just the dog. It was a metaphor for all the abjectivities
that existed: these were the forces that pulled us out
of ourselves, back into hell, back into the ground, back
into the pathology of others, and back into the political
and social bureaus. The snarling dog was no different

from any other of the facticities that threatened personal nihilation, and thus the encounter was disturbing. The sick taste in my mouth did not go away, even later when I was with friends, feeling incipient grief.

Later, I sat with half a beer in the dark contemplating the bizarre turn of events in my life. There was much to be said for a sedimented life—both negative and positive. Safety versus freedom was how I had constructed it, and I had grown comfortable with the way things were. Now I had a choice to return to what was, a memory that was not quite so clear; or I could remain, but the proviso was that my memory would eventually fade into nothingness until there was a black vacuum.

At first, I figured I would have nothing of it. I had been preparing to return to my point of origin, which filled me with such joy! But, alas, I was so attached here, and my heart was already bleeding in my imminent loss, such that I was ontologically compromised. I had been so trained in the dualisms of modernity that it was inconceivable that I could choose both; instead, I felt entirely caught on the horns of the dilemma, which— along with the grief—brought me such anxiety. So I set about to walking around town, undecided. I wondered if I could go forward and backward simultaneously.

I wandered around a great deal those days, heading up one street and down the next, going for a drive around the perimeter of the town, taking hikes into the hills, watching the movements of the clouds, and spending more and more time at the cemetery. The details of my life mattered less and less. What seemed more important were the existential decisions that involved mortality, transformation, and nihilating choices about my personal identity.

So much I had enjoyed my attachments and given them all up except for a wistful memory. So much I was enjoying my current attachments and had little desire to let them go. The fact that I felt less and less for the past in some sense disturbed me, like it somehow made less its importance.

I wondered if this would happen with my current holdings, which caused me great sadness, again as if their ephemeral nature made them less. Further, because the process of saying goodbye to the past was no different in kind that saying goodbye to the present—which would become past—it was logically impossible to choose. The only true difference is that the present had an advantage over the past, from my immediate temporal perspective. Upon further reflection, however, I discounted this last idea. That is, because I was able to enjoy the present and had for some time lived my current life narrative, I couldn't actually get to a transcendent position from which I could make the judgment.

During one of the nights the following week I had a difficult time getting to bed and even more of a difficult time falling asleep. When I did, I went down hard into the abyss, and entered into a strange world. I did not know if it was a dream. I had a part to play in a story—the plot of which does not matter—and I still do not know who was the scrivener. I woke several times with sweat then I re-entered the rabbit hole to a stage manager assigning parts to a story that was forced. Yet I played my part and came to enjoy it. When I felt myself being sucked up into the light of day, I fought like a tiger to stay. I wanted what I had! I was committed to it!

I'd changed.

And the clouds moved into twilight, dancing with the

wind as the sun started reeling its light back into its vault until morning like a fisherman reels his line. As I said, I awoke several times in the consideration of my temporal nature and the great angst I felt about the abyss between my deep past and my present attachments. The truth is that the notice of my imminent return had triggered a grave dilemma in me. I was effectively living in two places at once. I was two. This was not the *doppelganger* Dostoevski wrote about, or anything like that. It was worse because it involved two different temporal dimensions, and I had no idea how to bridge that disjunction.

As such, I started to consider what was the nature of this problem and what could be done to solve it, not just for me, but for anybody. For if we do not resolve the effects of past events, they stain the present. I was stained. However, it had the complication that [at least in my own mind] I was not responsible for my placement here, in this situation. In my own perception, this was not something that I would have chosen. Now that I had been given the chance to return, I found it very tempting, though this was not without substantial emotional cost—the loss of all the people I loved and who relied on me. And yet, it was tempting, this imperative to resolve the past. If I stayed I wondered if I could ever resolve it, and then this set me to thinking about how I'd do this if I didn't take care of the past by returning.

That led me to ponder the future. I'd been so indoctrinated into my current life that I hadn't examined the future other than as a necessary consequence of the past. I realized that there were three temporal dimensions, not two.

The future, as well, was a kind of indoctrination, one's focusing in it a distortion equal to reminiscing about the past. More specifically, directing one's intentional structure to the future seemed to be a type of return–no better than past directed. In my mind own mind I could see it as a movement from what is to what could be–from actual to possible. This included a comparison between the 'here and now' and the 'later and then.' The problem with this way of thinking was that by definition, the 'later and then' would never happen.

As such it was a murky nothingness, toward which nothing could ever really move. Yet I considered that I had come from the future and not the past, and thus the return was in the 'opposite' direction.

I continued driving by the cemetery with great regularity, noticing the uprooted weeds more and more with each pass. I was headed back.

9th Chapter

They had spent every last penny on drinking and smoking in the Mo Club again, and had done so since the old style bartender had cut them slack at sixteen. Occasionally they'd go fishing but they'd always bring too much beer and would come back drunk.

I'd first sat with them many years ago, and seeing them just the other day—a weekday—sliding out of the stools with whiskey breath at 3:00 p.m., was a reminder that some things don't change, ever. But I was on a quest to complete the three tasks involving a riddle, an artifact, and the unlearning, so seeing them again—it had been many years, collapsed my sense of temporality into one amorphous All and Everything, and brought me face to face with my youth, before I entered the Holograph and went on lifetime assignment.

They noticed me as they came out of the bar, and I could see by their facial expressions that they recognized me. "Hey, _____" they said, nodding. I nodded in return and replied. "Hey." That was all but it was an acknowledgement of our shared history in just a nod. Like I said, time collapsed in that moment. I never saw them again after that day and I didn't have to—the relationships completed themselves in the nod.

I ducked under a storefront and once inside, stopped at the post card rack, staring at one in particular that had 3 bullet points: *The Riddle, The Unlearning, and the Artifact!* It included a picture of the Valley with the three rivers meeting together in the sacred land. There were a few men in the back of the picture, and I was taken aback when I saw that one looked very much like me.

I hadn't wanted to talk to the men who I recognized because I wanted that part of my life over and done. After a few minutes when I thought the coast was clear I continued on my way and out to the back parking lot so I could get my car and go home. I still had a lot on my mind, figuring out whether I was going to return to the other world or not, since I had been given the choice. But there they were out in the lot, and I had still not figured out the significance of the riddle. The artifact told me nothing; and the "unlearning" was tying me in mental knots.

G_____ and J_____ were out in the lot leaning against their cars, talking in low voices and acknowledging me as I walked up. We engaged in pleasantries, made a few comments about the present, some about the past, and together watched the sun high in the sky, much as we had done many decades prior, though never becoming friends. Together we watched the sun, felt the light mountain breeze slap against our skin, and enjoyed the comfort of the land and our culture. The acknowledgement on the sidewalk from just a few minutes ago still stood—everything had completed, even the unfinished fistfight from high school and the unresolved slights from arrangements gone bad.

I'd never befriended these two, but even in that lack we were able to appreciate this land, and our time in it. We said our goodbyes, and I walked away, the postcard in my hand with the three tasks that I still didn't understand, which perplexed me further given that it was I who was in the picture. I felt a little edgy and unsettled with it, but drove home to the sanctity of my space.

On the way, I grabbed a newspaper at the mini-mart, got involved in a conversation with an old man on my block, and cut myself preparing a salad for dinner. I could taste the blood on the tomatoes.

The sun hung just a bit lower when I went out into the backyard to trim weeds, and then I flopped down into a chair for a while before dinner with the family.

After, I spoke on the telephone with an old friend—we'd taken a number of trips in the old Ford Fairlane together, and I could trust him with most of my private matters. Even though I started to tell him, in vague terms, about the intersection in my life, he launched into an arabesque about his daughter's marriage, a problem at work, and his new vacation house. I listened for a while but when it was my turn to talk, I was fatigued, and we ended the call.

A walk around the block, a night's sleep, and work in the morning set me onto an agreeable mood. On the way home, I drove by the mean dog on my way to the cemetery district of town, and noticed the dog wasn't there. I could see his chain but he wasn't there anymore. I could see the dirt where he'd lain.

I drove back and forth in front of the cemetery until a cop car passed by me, and I left because I didn't want to seem suspicious. I had been doing this more and more lately, at all hours of the day—sitting, walking—looking. With the rest of my life, I spent time with my family and my friends, acting in the same ways and doing the same things even though my inner reality was far, far away from all that was present. I was carrying the burden of being the Other.

I got involved with Friday Bingo at the Senior Center. This happened by chance when I was in their used-item store and got roped into it by one of the older workers who twisted my arm. This is not to say that I didn't enjoy it but I had some important things to think about.

Over the next weeks there were parties, and errands, and then a note came in the mail: I had 99 days to make a decision. I would either return at this time–the 100th day–or this option would be forever foreclosed. This served only to turn up the juice on my anxiety. I duly marked my calendar, noting each day until the reckoning, and then drove out to my favorite bar at the end of the week, having left work an hour early, and bellied up to the bar. I ordered nothing and settled on water with lemon.

By 5:30 p.m. I'd gotten myself into a savage and inane conversation about politics and then religion before things quickly turned to issues surrounding mortality. Several positions were expressed, reminding me only too well of my own choice I had to make, and because I didn't go in for the distraction, I left unfettered with drink.

Over the next many days, I was able to appreciate my waning hours, in this critical juncture. I wondered if I'd ever get the chance again should I not act on the dictum to return–it had been said that I wouldn't get the choice again.

There was the main avenue, which intersected with the main street.

There was the plateau that could flood.

There were the mountains in the background, watching.

There were the foothills, snuggled up against the original settlement.

I was the dirt here. I could always smell the rivers flowing together here in the meeting place.

I took comfort in the truth that one-way or the other if I stayed I'd fall into the earth here. My land. This was the core of my spirit: the land and the rivers meeting together, eroding each other, changing the course of everything politics and all.

I had been tracing and retracing my steps for a long time, crisscrossing my paths and intentionalities during each developmental step of the life I had chosen here.

I could smell the rivers in the morning when I'd go down there to look at the swirling transformations, sometimes including small whitecaps.

The years passed and occasionally I'd run into someone from another time period. Same face but usually very little emotional trigger.

New gravestones would appear intermittently. I'd walk the lanes and see the upturned earth.

It was easy to lose track of time.

99 days became 50, then 25. Then 9.

10th Chapter

The sun was warm like it had been then.

Agendas were pressed onto others; the only thing that changed was the faces and the context. Otherwise, it was the same.

The cracks in the sidewalk were never repaired even after many years. The bricks in the alley had all been rubbed clean by the patrons of the bars who came out to smoke, even in the winter. Decades of boots had worn down the crisp red to a dull, rounded sheen as the buildings received face lifts every quarter century or so. The same clouds came in on regular days when they became angry enough to crowd the sky.

The mountains stood ground. The hills were foot soldiers.

Worn down, dirt trails intermingled with tributaries of the rivers, bringing the last of the pulp remnants from the old paper mill downstream, past the town, down into the plateaus before rejoining the main current just outside.

A few old cars from the 40s and 50s inhabited a parking lot or two.

In the summers there were older cats sitting on porches; dogs roamed.

A steady flow of traffic came through, bleeding bigger ever year.

The snow receded a bit but the ski runs were still internationally known.

Scholars came in and out of town while the high schools processed class after class of the unruly and undisciplined.

The old woman tended her garden and ate the food people brought her. She expected this kind sort of treatment.

The letters on the hill, standing in for school names, withstood tough weather—wind and rain, and on occasion sleet and hail.

In the summers, little kinds drifted around in their neighborhoods kicking cans, playing little kid games that only they could understand, intoxicating themselves with the blue skies and the sun.

Cornstalks back in those days actually grew tall here, tall enough to produce good ears, but weather patterns had changed and so did the corn. This resulted in the smaller farmers to substitute in different crops with a shorter growing season.

Several of us left to go make our fortunes elsewhere, but many of these returned as their priorities changed and they reclaimed their relation to the land. And it was the land that held people together here: it was the land and the rivers coming together in this precious valley that was the stitching and the glue for everything else.

There were more motorcycles that came through here every year. You could hear them at all hours of the day and night, guttural, hard-grinding noises that those sorts of motorcycles make.

The houses in the old part of town–in the north side–still stood, strong, like deer in a field they'd claimed, chewing the grass of their lives no matter the consequence, sucked gently into their own abjectivity–completely authentic. They were like cousins to the older foothills that bordered them–solidarity.

On occasion, tourists pointed out the horizontal furrows that cut across the hills, close to the top. These were deep cuts that you could see from several miles away. The glacial lake was still here in spirit, having spilt blood from the mountain, not that it would ever heal: it was more like a blood brother, joined in the pain and suffering witnessed since the water had receded, making way for the humans to dance. So far, the lake had not returned, its veins found only in the moving liquid of the rivers.

An old saloon door was in his basement.

Dresses from the whores were stuffed in boxes, hidden.

The ornamented building front was still there even though someone had tried to paint over it.

Fire ants continued to claim the scrub and sagebrush out on the plateaus, even though folks tried to burn them out every summer.

And the wind continued to blow everything and everyone back in, all in due time.

The 9 days dwindled to 3, and then I decided to release myself from the schedule. I'd had enough of the Proctors and the Consortium of Rules.

If only–

If only—

If only—

I almost hit a home run that year. It could have been from the new eyeglasses but I think it was more about squaring off with reality, running alongside being until it tired of being chased and gave in to love.

It might have been when I was eleven when they built the newest cemetery, to "accommodate more," someone said. It was up on a hill instead of down in town, down in the valley of the town, and as such the town seemed smaller. From there you could see where the rutted out dirt roads where kids drove to smoke and drink. You could feel their hearts pressed into the dirt just by being out there.

I wanted to be the dirt out here. Precious dirt.

Intermittent with my attempts to give myself a break from my big decision came my dream of the smallish white house with the porch. I wanted the porch and neighbors I'd quibble with, and my bones to sink into the floorboards until we both rotted together.

Then it was the last day, and a note came explaining that I had to appear to report on the riddle, the artifact, and the unlearning. This was prelude to the expectation that I'd comply.

"If only," he said one last time as I walked out of his office a free man.

THIRD PART

11th Chapter

We'd watched the green grass together in the middle of the field. He thought it was "almost heaven." That was 29 years ago, just a few seasons before he passed away into the land. Now I was close to the age he'd been when he died, and figured I still had a few things to do before my own day.

When I was in town we would sit in his back yard and watch the mountains to the west. Over the years the trees he'd planted had grown so much that there was little space left to see out, but when we could, I'd always notice the misty fog sitting at the top of the two mountains that came together near the top. In fact, I'd always dreamed of hiking up there, that getting to the top would bring me a kind of wisdom that I perceived myself as lacking. So, we would sit and look up there, sometimes not saying anything–just looking.

The time had gone fast: time through childhood; time building dreams; time living them; time destroying them. I'd imagined this time, when I'd be reminiscing about my life and reminiscing about him. I knew three decades ago what this would be like, and in fact it was no different from what I imagined. That is, the experience in my mind and the experience in fact were the same, so closely aligned that they would collapse into one experience–an authentic convergence between actuality and possibility.

His words oscillated between sarcastic-humorous quips and precious wisdoms, so I would always listen carefully, hungry for his sagacity. And every year in the last years he'd threaten not to plant a garden but he always would. This is where I thought he'd pass on—out in the garden—but it happened inside on a break. He just sat down, sweat rolling off his forehead, leaned back. His mouth opened as if he had started to drift into a deep sleep. Then he passed away, the sprinklers full blast, the grass particularly green and the garden planted. It would be a good harvest in the fall.

After he died, everything changed in my world, and I realized that I had to take more responsibility for my life or I wouldn't accomplish what I needed to, so I would spend much of my time walking around town having this dialogue with him even though he wasn't there. It would always start with a "What do you think of this?" More cogently I'd turn to look at him as a way to get his opinion but he wasn't there. I'd just be talking to thin air.

Thus I continued walking and aging, occasionally running into people I used to know, retracing old steps on familiar paths, understanding that I was getting older; I could tell that I was getting old because of the way my tempo had slowed.

Just before he died, I bought a place in the old neighborhood, which I think pleased and delighted him. It was a stone's throw from where I'd grown up, and I knew all the streets. I felt a belonging—not a sense of belonging—but a true belonging. This earth; this dirt; these streets; the memories from my youth had captured me, forcing me back into the abjectivity of my history.

Yet, it was a sweet capture. Safe. Pristine like pure-white snowfields; like the salvation that comes from two days of rain.

From my new house, I could see the place where I grew

up, but from a different angle and a different view. It allowed me a new perspective, not only about the land but also about my past—an uncovering of the secret and deceptive veils that we weave to cover our fragile parts. Now, at my own 11th hour, preparing for my departure and my return into the land that I had grown to love, I was able to laugh at all my foolishness, and all my mistakes. It seems that the more I tried to run away from the truth of who I was, the more that truth emerged into the world, into my own consciousness.

Being back home now afforded me the luxury of my memories: sweet, sad, some horrible, joyous, all of the complicating elements that go into making life from beginning to end. I'd made choices fully intended, and would have been worse off had I substituted "rationality" for "authenticity." I owned my choices, and I own them now, late into the game. And I continued to walk and to retrace old steps.

Baseball diamonds. Parks. Rivers. Trails. Coffee shops. The houses that formerly belonged to friends. Family members. Restaurants where we'd met. The hills. The mountains. The cemeteries. I'd still drive by and look inside the black, wrought iron fence, apparently searching for some kind of movement that never came, save for the delicate breeze that would puff itself up and roll over the headstones lining the rows and rows and rows.

But no one was there that I could see, and sometimes I'd park—walk around some more. I'd go inside the wrought iron and read the stones, delighted when I saw someone I used to know, even though perhaps I'd done this before, and again and again.

The dirt here owned me, and I realized again and over that I'd sensed all this a long time ago. I was living the same life, just from a different temporal perspective. I had the small white house with the porch now, alone except for a dog I had acquired. I would sit there and think as old men do, watching the sun go from east to west, and then watching some more until it sat and went down into dusk, into the night.

Almost everyone I knew in the early days was gone—had either left or died, and the people I knew in the present knew little of what had come before. My inner experience, therefore, was so much more than what I showed, and I figured it must be reciprocal in those I saw.

I kept waiting for something to happen. It could have been anything; something out of the norm; something big; anything—but it never happened. Everything just was, moving in accordance with its internal coherence, but this finally taught me that what was, was already here. No one came home from wherever they had gone to; the dead stayed in the ground. And I walked and reminisced.

Sometimes I'd go to the church I'd been raised in to see if someone I used to know would show up, or if I might gain some special insight or wisdom, but no one came and I learned nothing.

Pure time had destroyed my learning.

I was already dead and had been for some time.

I had nothing new to say.

12th Chapter

I imagine he thought it was all bullshit—a fiction
that someone fabricated in order to run a game on
everyone. He'd still have none of it. It was, as he would
say "the program."

This is why he was so quiet unless challenged.

This is why he'd venture little unless asked.

Fiction! It was just plain fiction.

Made up stories and values, truths and myths. Fiction.

Claims and ways. Fiction!

And now he was gone. They had put him in the ground
with the contraption.

He had waved at me from the edge of the cemetery on
the knoll.

We had spoken together near the mountain lake.

He'd always offered me solace.

And now he was gone, and I was older with gray hair
and a faulty memory.

*The walking hurt my knees but I continued. There was
something I was searching for; something I had to find.
I'd poke around old places and take notes—I recorded
everything, and I ended up in campgrounds and
streams outside of town, trying to follow directions he'd*

given me a long time ago.

I was retracing his steps—and mine, in the hopes of finding the lost messages—the wisdom that was passed but for which I had not been ready. Thus I would return to my memory of him, walking the red road until the passing of all things.

I'd sit on the white porch and feel the west wind on my face. This was the red road.

I'd walk the grass until I was tired. This was the red road.

Three generations back I could remember, and three forward, which is six—and me in the middle joining the winds of the west, east, north, and south; pondering the above and imagining the below. Joining all, and me in the middle, walking the red road. All else, and all dreams fell away in a series of traumas, joys, holdings and release. The sun fell across my brow, the sweat dripping down my forehead.

I would continue my walking for several more years before my dog died. He was my third, very patient with my age, served me faithfully without any regret or complaint. I sincerely believed that I would meet all three—together—at the waiting station, a bridge, and then go forward into the unknown. I also believed this about everyone else with whom I'd shared love.

It was this Gaze of the Other—a non-possessory, loyal projection—that had animated the deepening of my commitments, and my faithful companions, like my father, had brought me into new levels of awareness of what was already present.

His water bowl I cleaned and shelved. His lease with the other two made three. The pictures and the paw prints I

would hold until last breath, along with the earlier ones—
no loss from time. The evening, after I did what I had
to do—I couldn't bear him to suffer further, I sat on the
white porch just like I did in a repetitive dream that I'd
had since I was a young man.

I had already lived this life.

I had already been here through a portal from one
temporal zone to another.

I was already both dead and alive at the same time.

When I had cried long enough, I put all the pictures of
all of them, everyone I had known and loved, and any
similar artifact—anything—on a large table. I left them all
out there for days. I would look at them and remember.
I'd feel.

I did this for several weeks in between my walks and
the writing. I still had a number of projects to finish, and
I would. It was a necessary phase of my destiny, that
transition from the 11th hour to the 12th, along with the
arrangements on the knoll.

I'd be there amongst them, overlooking the plateaus
and the hills to the west, and down in the old part of
the city where I was living, close to the original city
cemetery. My plan was to burn a bit of everything and
collect the ashes into an urn, which would be mixed
with my own—and others—then spread onto my place
in both cemeteries, as well as thrown into a certain part
of the river where I'd played as a boy, and then some
buried in the sacred mountain area near the misty top. I
had been thinking about this for over fifty years.

My memory got worse but my plan was intact. I made
more trips to the cemetery near where I lived, walking,

walking. I would talk to the spirits of those I had loved, and I talked to all of my companions, each at just the right time. And I walked, retracing my steps, thinking about the choices; feeling no longer any kind of weight but instead a relief of a life lived well; it was a life of goodness.

I no longer had any attachment to any particular version of the truth of my life or anything else for that matter. I realized that I [we] [had] spent my whole life making truth claims and value claims, incessantly, until we exhausted ourselves—only to later relax our grip on it late. At this point, I knew it was soon finished and that it was—still was—joy beyond comprehension. Reminiscing was like tasting a fine meal and dessert late into the night, divided in both wanting it to end and not. In the end, cleansing one's palette made the enjoyment so much more profound. In short, it was good to die, as long it was a good death—the culmination of a life lived on the red road.

Questions of authenticity—the "who" questions—were false; red herring problems that resulted in nothing, no wisdom, no comfort, nothing. Relaying such matters was even more complicated, ultimately an even more mangled and complex story—with multiple interpretations and perspectives. Like the difference between the actual and the possible, these ideals of return and homecoming were all petty lies, inoculations against the freedom of space and time.

13th Chapter

I woke up in a graveyard leaning up against a red maple tree on the downside of a hill. Because it was almost summer I was not cold, and the robins dancing in the grass spoke to me in tones I'd not heard since childhood.

I didn't move but instead allowed my mind to wander. It was quiet—except for the birds—which gave me the presence of mind to both enjoy my immediate surroundings but also to indulge my imagination.

There were many temptations in life I had finally come to see, not necessarily "bad" things or "wrong" things, but things, sometimes good ones, that pull us off our course; I had learned that it was very difficult to say no to good things—to people, places, and ideas that were alluring. On the other hand, simple circumspection—ratiocination—could cut through this pull in consciousness, but it required the creation of division between the temptation and the destiny. This is what I had been doing for several years in order to maintain clarity and destiny. It hurt more but the clarity and precision were tempting in their own right.

Eventually, I opened my eyes fully as the sun moved into the eastern sky just above the entrance to this lush valley, to the canyon that had opened itself to a glacier 17,000 years earlier.

The grass was wet, it was late spring, and I rubbed both hands on either side until they were laden with precipitation. I was then able to wipe my face until it felt fresh—a little more so because of the light breeze that

61

had started to swirl up and into the place.

For a while it was quiet, though I could hear an auto or two a few blocks away, probably heading out this Saturday morning for groceries and errands. A few robins started dancing on the grassy hill, making their usual sounds, clucking around looking for worms.

I didn't move though I did stretch out to create a different angle between my back and the tree trunk, repositioning my legs until they were fully stretched out before me.

Eventually, an old truck drove up into the place, inside the black, wrought-iron gate, onto the dirt lanes until it stopped no more than thirty feet from me. A man got out, appeared not to notice me, and went about to his chores near the water supply. In the forty-five minutes that he was there, before he got into the truck and drove away to the grounds building, he had to have seen me. But he said nothing and did not acknowledge me.

By then—it must have been mid-morning—the grass had started to dry, and the sun had poked its way through the canyon opening to the east, pushing heat and light into the valley. The robins had somehow gotten their fill and by now were gone, leaving me with the unnoticing groundskeeper puttering in his work shed. There was the blue sky and the quiet, along with a light breeze and more noise coming from the town. It was the weekend.

I eventually got on my feet and started walking around, bending down to inspect each stone for the name, always looking for a message, which I would catalogue in my mind. I walked around for a while, first staying to the narrow packed-dirt lane then deviating into the grass, which separated the stones and the names.

First one and then another caught my attention: Something about the name was familiar but I couldn't place it. It was like almost remembering something that was on the cusp of presencing but wouldn't. I stood motionless, somewhat paralyzed–or caught rather, in the interstitial space waiting for the inchoate thought. However, it wouldn't come and eventually I continued rambling around the place, curious why the groundskeeper didn't acknowledge me.

I lost interest in it when a parade of cars showed up, passing through the gate to a tent that had been set up to the west I started drifting quietly to the southern edge of it. I found an opening, slipped through, and stood alone at the outside edge, in the southeast corner, while more cars arrived.

By now the day was hot, the sun illuminating everything, and I decided to leave there. By now the grass was dry, and many were accumulating around the tent area, the groundskeeper still working on something just in the front of his shed. I started walking, briefly scanning the old baseball diamond across the street. For the first time, I thought it odd that the city would build a baseball park across the street from a cemetery. They still played games there but not as much as in the past. Weeds grew a bit more on the sides than I could remember–and the outlines of the infield were hazier than they used to be, like in a dream perhaps.

So, I walked, first around the cemetery but then back again to the street between it and the baseball field. As the sun rose higher in the sky, late spring-early summer, I set out toward town, several blocks away.

I took a southerly direction walking at a leisurely pace,

past one block then another, until I could see the cars zipping past me in both directions, left to right, and right to left. This street, Toole, was a dividing line, and had been here nearly from the town's origin. It represented the difference between the old part of town and the new: it was almost like two towns. Once across, I felt the change: different tempo, a different feel, maybe because the city streets had bigger and better curbs; the people were slightly better groomed with clothing that seemed to fit with the season and the times; and there was a sense of belonging that manifested itself in more communication flow, familiarity in greeting, and non-verbal gesturing openness.

Folks from the north were perhaps treated as outsiders even though they were actually insiders, born from the stock of the original settlers here. What was original was actually Other. I kept on going straight ahead, walking past Toole all the way to the main street that was perpendicular to it. I took a left heading east, moving slowly but deliberately shaking the grit off my clothes and the perspiration from my face.

I was in town now and headed for the diner. He and I used to spend a great deal of time there, a long time ago before he passed. There was a seat in the back.

14th Chapter

I walked so much my feet started to hurt everyday. When he was younger we would walk together, traversing a number of older streets and trails that people no longer used much. Red brick and packed dirt—with new perspectives for me, and which engendered conversation.

I sold one car and gave the other away, then used my bike until it was trashed, which left me with the bus and the walking. I chose walking in most cases unless it was the dead of winter. Then I'd take the bus.

Sometime we'd take coffee with us; mostly it was just the walk along with the talking: This would include family matters, politics and religion, and our philosophical contemplations about life.

Here's how it would go: "Nice day today—gonna be warm."

"Yep, blue skies."

Then there might be conversation about something happening in town—usually involving the law, a crime, and what the newspaper said. And try as I might, I wouldn't get much from him other than a question or two, asking me my opinion about it.

Today it was warm and the skies blue. Yesterday I had gone over up on the north side of town just walking around, looking at the porches, crossing past the wrought iron.

I walked all the way from the river near where I'd grown up. This was at least three miles, but I'd walked these streets so often I knew every trail, curb, tree, house, dog, and cat. But I always learned a new perspective, due to a slightly different sky with different lighting, and the angle of my phenomenological body in space, hunched forward in time.

Today was no exception. I had gotten up early, consumed quite a bit of coffee and was now out and about—walking around town. I'd started midtown, sky open, robins appearing and then disappearing, the asphalt heating, heels sore.

I made it out to the Bitterroot by noon and watched the small eddies form on the sides next to the driftwood, little vanilla ice-cream tops forming then dissipating, some of it accumulating next to the bank. I used to come out here with my dog, and with him. I could still see him crouching down to point out something he'd seen across the river, and I could never match him in awareness. Instead of focusing on matters that were far away, or past or future, he was able to focus on our immediate experience.

I would watch him do this, and had from the beginning— and over the years my quizzical reaction finally led to a smile. I came to realize that he was wholly in the world with all of his being. He was so fully in his experience— not in the midst of it, but totally in it—that he didn't need to concern himself with what had happened or with what might be.

After spending some time out here in the thicket that abutted the river, I took the narrow trail back to the road, and walked step by step until I was back in town.

"The man who dies before he dies. . . ." [I continued with

this line over and over in my end, twisting it into new expressions.]

"The man who doesn't die before he dies, . . . dies when he dies."

What was death? I don't know. In fact, I didn't know much of anything—maybe some of the mundane—the usual and the easy, but I didn't really know anything of import. Words would often fail me, and my memory worsened. Where was I going? I don't know. What did I learn in this life? I don't know. Nothing was clear-cut, and my beliefs had changed continuously. As far as the city knew I was just another citizen: I had tried hard to stay within the white line. As far as my family knew, I was a prodigal son.

Had I returned? I don't think so. Had I come back to myself? I don't know what that meant. I do know that I had spent most of a lifetime trying to fill in gaps and holes and other interstitial corridors. I'd learned absolutely nothing, and my fantasies seemed to rule my behavior and my overall attitude toward everything. Yes, of course, I was attached to people and ideas and things, but the most important ones I had buried— somewhere safe and somewhere protected within the fiber of my heart, my consciousness.

"The riddle, the artifact, and the unlearning."

I continued walking around town until the sun waned and the air chilled. I tried to make it back to my place on the north side, up past Toole, past the point of needing forgiveness, until I made it up there near the old schoolhouse, not too far from the cemetery.

There I took off my boots, cooked up some lean meat and vegetables, and sat on the porch turning ideas around in my mind until the sun slowly sank between the hills and the mountains to the west, and it became dusk, then dark.

The air turned tepid and then chilly—no breeze of any kind, just the coldness. It was dark on the porch except for the lamp I had hanging off the one side. Otherwise, some of the warmth of my little abode leaked out from behind the screen door.

My belly was warm, my feet sore, carefully wrapped in soft-woolen socks, a cup of hot tea in front of me. I was tired and old, and had little to do the morrow except for my walking. I am sure there were places I had to go, but I'd worry about that when the sun came up.

I finished my tea and listened to barking dogs, cars coming home from wherever, and sunk a bit into the chair. I was tired. My parents, brothers, sister, family, friends, acquaintances, and colleagues were all dead—I'd outlived all of them. Like I said earlier, this is not to say that I didn't know people, but these were all new and newer, and they didn't know me except as being an old man in the neighborhood.

As I drifted off to sleep I reminisced about the decision I'd made many, many years ago in a far away place. I'd made the decision to return home. And I did.

15th Chapter

I was sequestered in the knoll on the hill while the rituals were being played out in town. I was told that I had a choice: I could either allow my burial to complete itself and rest forever here in the dirt of this fertile valley; or I could choose to return to my spiritual origin, a place I could hardly remember except with fantastical, imaginary fragments of experience.

They came up here in the afternoon—a Sunday—driving slowly, tears angling down drawn, tired cheeks, a number of them wearing black. It was a somber mood, I could tell, especially from the lack of words; it was mostly gestures and glances.

When the indigo-blue Fairlane came from the opposite direction—the west hills and the Bitterroot River—I could see it was him so I smiled. He'd always cut his own path, even if it were harder than the usual and the obvious. When the old car rounded the bend coming up the hill, and dodged into the parking lot, I felt a warm awareness of my solidarity with him. We were a lot alike, cut from the same spiritual cloth and though we had different lives, saw most things the same way. I was the apple and he the tree.

I looked around me at the green, quiet lawns while they continued to arrive. I rotated my body in a circle, taking in the expansive view of the valley, the hills, and the mountains, parts of the undulating river system peeking out from various thickets of forest, the rest of it winding through town.

It was sunny today—blue skies and warm air, and I drank

it in. The grass had been freshly cut and the parking lot was immaculate, the edges trimmed precisely so you could easily see the boundary between the parking of the living and the grassy hill of the dead. However, both overlooked the plateau and the hills to the west, and the buildings in the east—in unison—set apart only by time.

I breathed fully, slowly, taking in a mixture of tears, sun, warmth, and the fatigue of a lifetime. My muscles were still sinewy from exercise, my body strong from use, and my spirit light but focused. I considered my options.

I'd always been a philosophical owl, staying late to protect the innocent, outliving the others from my generation, a Night Watchman, and a curator of souls. I'd made numerous mistakes in my life, far too many too count, or remember, but I'd always recovered and I'd always landed on my feet. But I was tired, having played out the hand.

Such a beautiful hand it was, replete with vulnerability and an occasional trump card—just enough to motivate the new.

And it was the new that pushed me forward, that raw experience of the frontier, transcending actuality continuously in order to live in that narrow corridor that separated us from possibility. And it was so familiar to me.

Nobody saw me. They were too busy weeping. Nobody heard me humming as my eyes roamed the skies, noticing a hawk, imagining a rabbit below. I held many questions still, and was unsure that I had learned anything. My memory was so fragmented and all.

I had pressed on for so many years, anticipating

a return, then forgetting it, despising it, loving it, cherishing it—going through an oscillation of attachment and release, holding and letting go, my fidelity winning out for the duration. And here they were, my funeral, my family, these people of mine. And I was at another intersection—the one that would not be outstripped by any other—so it seemed.

I had been taught to believe that there was an origin from which all things come, from which I had been spawned in body, mind, and heart. I had learned to attach so deeply to this belief that all derivatives and substitutes never measured closely. And I judged everything in terms of the distance between where I was and where I thought this beginning point might be located.

To be sure, before me now was the chance to return again, to enjoy even for a few minutes the suffering that could come only from appreciating this distance between what was and the penumbra of the past or the speculations of tomorrow.

I was no longer certain to what I would be returning. I could not tell what they would be like—all of them—and whether they would still be there waiting.

Waiting. Waiting. Waiting.

The hawk flew away.

The pastor had arrived.

I had the choice: I was at the crossroads.

During the words, which ebbed and flowed, the volume rising and falling, closing and receding, a stranger or two making their way across the lawn, late, quietly.

Try as I might I could not see anymore where it was that I had thought was home. These people, I wasn't sure anymore, whether they had known me, and now I realize that it hadn't mattered anyway.

The ghost of a little dog ran across me heading into the field; one I had know a long time ago, moving too fast to catch or even touch. My memories were failing me seriously, and I grasped for them in vain—and in a moment a number of things occurred.

Clouds formed.

A baby was born. It looked like me someone said.

I made my choice, and into the dirt I went, along with the coffin. My son saw me standing at the edge of the knoll, and in the moment he took to wipe a tear from his eyes, I entered into the earth. I chose the dirt. I welcomed the abjectivity of it, the pulsing of the life around me, tears and sweat, and the dark mood: I could tell that afternoon had just crested.

After they dispersed, later, I felt dirt cascading over me, in my face, weighting me to the earth, this land of mine, and I welcomed it like sun and air.

POST
SCRIPT

16th Chapter

Only a few years later, someone tore down the baseball field next to the other cemetery.

17th Chapter

Later, two boys would play in that city cemetery, not the one on the knoll, but the one down in the valley, in the north side where they lived. Their last name was on a number of stones, which intrigued them to no end, one saying the words:

De tout mon coeur.

Another,

Toujours.

The dirt.

Look for the companion novel:

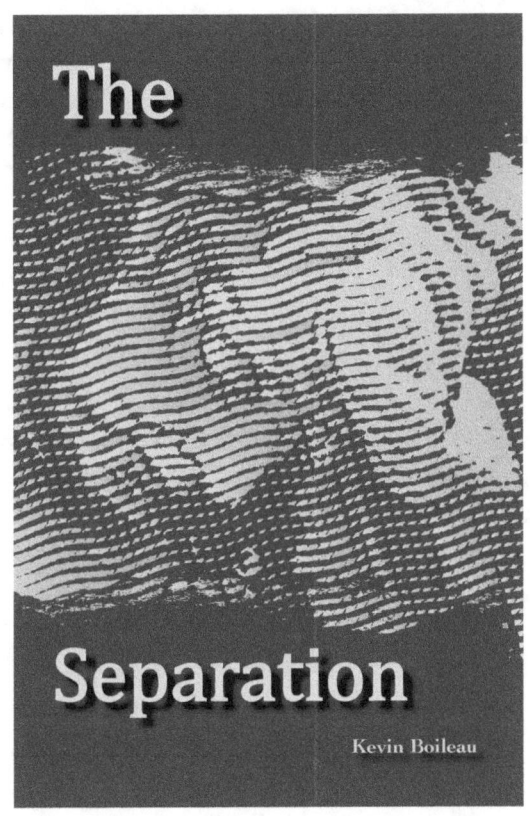

HEART-OF-FIRE

Heart-of-Fire is an imprint of EPIS Press dedicated solely to fiction, poetry, and other literary production that is related to psychoanalysis, phenomenology, and Critical Theory/ deconstruction.

EPIS Press
31 Fort Missoula Road
Suite 4
Missoula, MT 59804
epispublishing1@gmail.com
www.episworldwide.com

www.ingramcontent.com/pod-product-compliance
Lightning Source LLC
Chambersburg PA
CBHW070606180626
46817CB00005B/2021